This picture book is inspired by a true story.

ÉGALITÈ

I Love My Colorful Nails
Egalité Series

© Text: Alicia Acosta and Luis Amavisca, 2018
© Illustrations: Gusti, 2018
© Edition: NubeOcho, 2019
www.nubeocho.com · hello@nubeocho.com

Original title: *¡Vivan las uñas de colores!*
English translation: Ben Dawlatly
Text editing: Rebecca Packard

Distributed in the United States by
Consortium Book Sales & Distribution

Second edition: may 2019
First edition: april 2019
ISBN: 978-84-17123-59-8

Printed in Portugal.

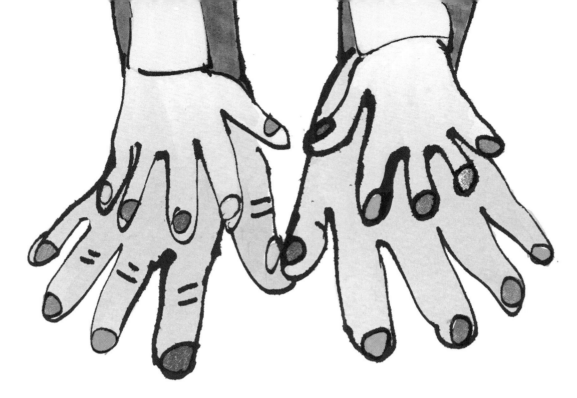

I LOVE MY COLORFUL NAILS

ALICIA ACOSTA
LUIS AMAVISCA

ILLUSTRATED BY GUSTI

nubeOCHO

Ben loves painting his nails. More than anything, he likes to paint them with cheerful colors. As cheerful as him.

When they're painted, he likes picking things up just to look at his hands and enjoy how colorful and fun they look.

Why does Ben paint his nails?
It's simple. There's no mystery to it:

He does it because he loves his colorful nails.

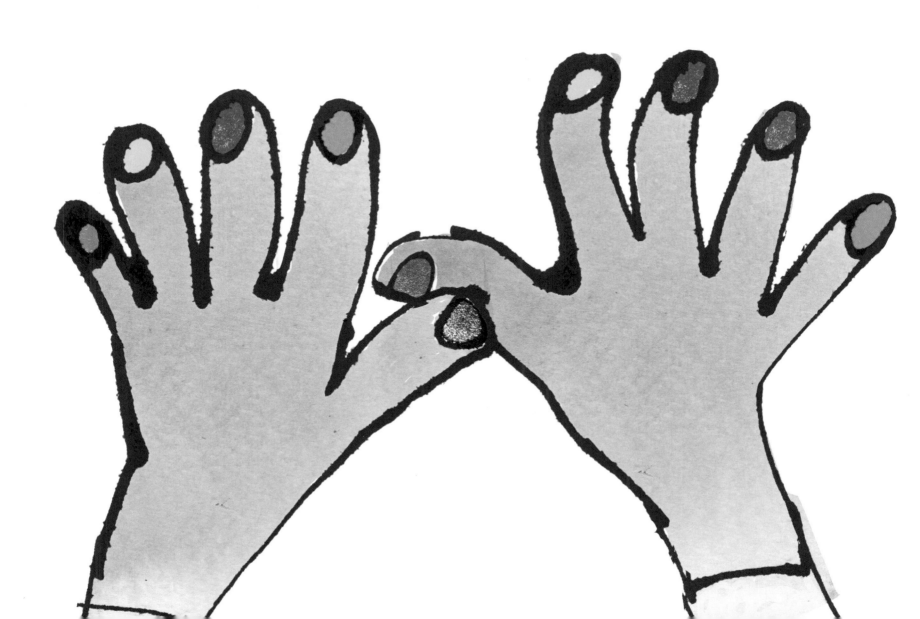

Most afternoons, once Ben finishes his homework,
he asks his mommy for her collection of nail polishes.
She has a boxful! They're really pretty.
Mommy loves sharing them.

His friend Margarita also has amazing nail polishes. Whenever they can, they paint their nails together.

"Green with brown? Too sad!"

"Yellow and pink? No way!"

"Pistachio and orange! A match made in heaven!"

One morning, Ben had his nails painted a delightful bright red. He had just stepped into school, when two boys started teasing him.

"Painting your nails is for girls."
"You're a girl! You're a girl!"

Ben felt terrible. He couldn't understand why they would tease him. He was even sadder than the day when he lost his ball or when he dropped his three-scoop ice cream on the floor.

So a couple of days later, he told his mommy and daddy all about it.

Daddy said in a serious tone of voice,
"Ben, I'm also a boy and do you know what?

We're going to paint our nails!
I'll have orange, please!"

But at school a few days later, there were now three boys laughing at Ben and saying mean things to him.

"Only girls do that!"
"Ben is a girly girl! Ben is a girly girl!"

Ben got even more upset. He couldn't understand why they'd do that. He felt even sadder than the day his fish went to fishy heaven.

"Leave him alone!" shouted Margarita.

From that moment on, Ben would only paint his nails on the weekend. On Sunday afternoons, he would ask Mommy to remove the nail polish, even if it was his favorite color.

His nails were no longer bright and cheerful. Neither was Ben. But he didn't want the kids at school to laugh at him again.

Daddy, on the other hand, would go to pick Ben up from school every day with his nails painted and a huge smile on his face, although the huge smile was nothing new.

A week later it was Ben's birthday.

This year it was on a Monday, and like every Monday, Ben went to school with no nail polish on. He would have liked to have painted his nails bright blue.

Oh how he loved bright blue!

With their hands up in the air, they all shouted,

"HAPPY BIRTHDAY, BEN!"

That birthday, Margarita got Ben a bottle of dazzling sky blue nail polish.

And at recess, the whole class painted each other's nails in all the bright, cheerful colors... cheerful just like Ben.

Without a doubt, this was the birthday of his dreams.

Who could ask for anything else?